W9-BMY-918

THE FOOT WARMER AND THE CROW

EVELYN COLEMAN
illustrated by DANIEL MINTER

MACMILLAN PUBLISHING COMPANY NEW YORK
MAXWELL MACMILLAN CANADA TORONTO
MAXWELL MACMILLAN INTERNATIONAL NEW YORK OXFORD SINGAPORE SYDNEY

 Macmillan Publishing Company is part of the Maxwell Communication Group of Companies. Macmillan Publishing Company, 866 Third Avenue, New York, NY 10022. Maxwell Macmillan Canada, Inc., 1200 Eglinton Avenue East, Suite 200, Don Mills, Ontario M3C 3N1. First edition. Printed in Hong Kong by South China Printing Company (1988) Ltd.
The text of this book is set in 14 pt. Leawood Medium. The illustrations are painted wood carvings.
10 9 8 7 6 5 4 3 2 1

Library of Congress Cataloging-in-Publication Data
Coleman, Evelyn, date. The foot warmer and the crow / Evelyn Coleman ; illustrated by Daniel Minter. — 1st ed. p. cm. Summary: A patient slave finally wins his freedom through his own cleverness and the advice of a crow. ISBN 0-02-722816-9 [1. Slavery—Fiction. 2. Afro-Americans—Fiction.] I. Minter, Daniel, ill. II. Title. PZ7.C6746Fo 1994 92-38352 [E]—dc20

To my mother, Annie S. Coleman,
who taught me that "our survival of
enslavement is all the testament
we need of our greatness,"
and to every child who needs
to empower themselves,
I offer the spirit of Hezekiah
—E. C.

To Brian and Spencer
—D. M.

Long ago, in the time of shackles and slavery, there lived an enslaved man called Hezekiah. For many years, he worked long and hard with the sun baking his brow and his back bent to the ground, planting and harvesting the plantation fields. There he labored, until he was won by a slave owner named Master Thompson as part of a wager.

When Master Thompson spied Hezekiah among his newly won possessions, his usual scowl turned into a smile, because in that moment he decided exactly what he would do with Hezekiah.

You see, Hezekiah had grown to be a man in his heart, but he was not a man in size. Master Thompson knew nothing of heart, being a bully himself, and so was only amused by Hezekiah's smallness.

At parties, Master Thompson pulled Hezekiah out like a deck of playing cards. "Come on out here, boy, and dance a jig. Watch him, he can stand on his head. Why, he can even do flips! Go on! Jump, boy!"

However, if for any reason the guests were not amused, Master Thompson beat poor Hezekiah. So, having wit and wisdom, Hezekiah soon became the most amusing slave in those parts. And eventually the master grew fond of him.

But Hezekiah held hidden knowledge in his heart of hearts. For he could commune with the birds. He whistled such beautiful and enchanting songs that birds large and small perched on his shoulders and whispered their secrets, past and present, into his ears.

Over time, as the birds lifted in flight from Hezekiah's shoulders, they stirred his own desire for freedom. One day, Hezekiah made up his mind: He could not be enslaved any longer. He would be free like the birds, or die trying.

One mild summer night, Hezekiah sneaked away with only the glow of the moon to light his path. He knew freedom lay to the north, one full night and day's journey from the plantation.

Hezekiah's short legs scrambled as fast as they could through the woods. Thorns and bushes tore at his clothes. He grabbed snarled branches to pull himself through the swamp mud. And he waded, as slow as molasses in winter, among the alligators; all to reach the free man's crossing. But still, when the sun peeked its head from behind the night's clouds, Hezekiah heard the dogs barking, hot on his trail.

He quickly hid, but the dogs had already picked up his scent. Before the sun could rise any higher, Hezekiah lay huddled under a bush, surrounded by dogs and men.

The slave master was so angry with Hezekiah that steam poured from his nostrils. He yelled in a booming voice, "How dare you run away after I've been so good to you!" He and his men whipped Hezekiah all the way back to the plantation. For a time after, Master Thompson treated Hezekiah even more cruelly and kept close watch on his doings until he felt confident Hezekiah would not dare run away again.

But the desire for freedom still swelled in Hezekiah's soul. He could not remain enslaved much longer.

Then one night, while the fireflies sparkled through the warm air, a crow flew onto Hezekiah's shoulder. The crow told him a tale of Master Thompson as a child. "When I was not even fully feathered, your master found me and my brothers and sisters in our nest in a tree. He took us down, ignoring our caws of fear. When our mother spotted him, she swooped down upon him to protect us from harm. She pecked and pulled at his face and hair. But your master took a stick and knocked her to the ground. Then he used that same stick to punch out her eyes. He came back, day after day, to see my helpless brothers and sisters die. I was the only nestling to survive."

Hezekiah listened and understood. The crow then craned his neck to look deep into Hezekiah's eyes, where a man's true longings are always revealed. The crow took his leave, but not before he whispered to Hezekiah, "You must learn all you can about your master and use his weaknesses to your advantage. Then you will know how to be free."

In the following weeks, Hezekiah studied Master Thompson carefully, day and night, just as the crow had suggested.

The first thing Hezekiah learned was that the master would bet on anything. He would even wager on an enslaved person's life. And then one day Hezekiah overheard some of the cooks laughing. "The master talks all night long in his sleep," they whispered.

So by the time winter stalked, attacking the plantation with snow and ice, Hezekiah had come up with a plan. First, he offered to become Master Thompson's foot warmer. On those bitter nights, when even the water in the washbasin froze over, Hezekiah snuggled around the master's feet, keeping them warm. Hezekiah stayed alert under the smelly covers, listening intently to his master's rantings and ravings through the night.

In the daylight hours, while the sap thawed, Hezekiah sneaked short naps and dreamed of one day having his freedom. He vowed once again that he would be free like the birds, or die trying.

A few months before the big spring auction, when the enslaved people were herded together and traded or sold like animals, the crow flew once again onto Hezekiah's shoulders. "What have you learned of your master, old friend?" he asked.

Hezekiah shared his knowledge and his plan with the crow. The crow nodded in quiet satisfaction and flew up and away.

The very next day, Hezekiah approached Master Thompson.

"Master, I know something you think no one knows."

"You're just a slave. What could you know?"

"I know you want to trade John, the slave, 'cause you think your daughter has taken a liking to him."

The master's mouth flew open and his eyes bulged out.

Each day as the big auction approached, Hezekiah revealed one secret after another from the slave master's hidden thoughts.

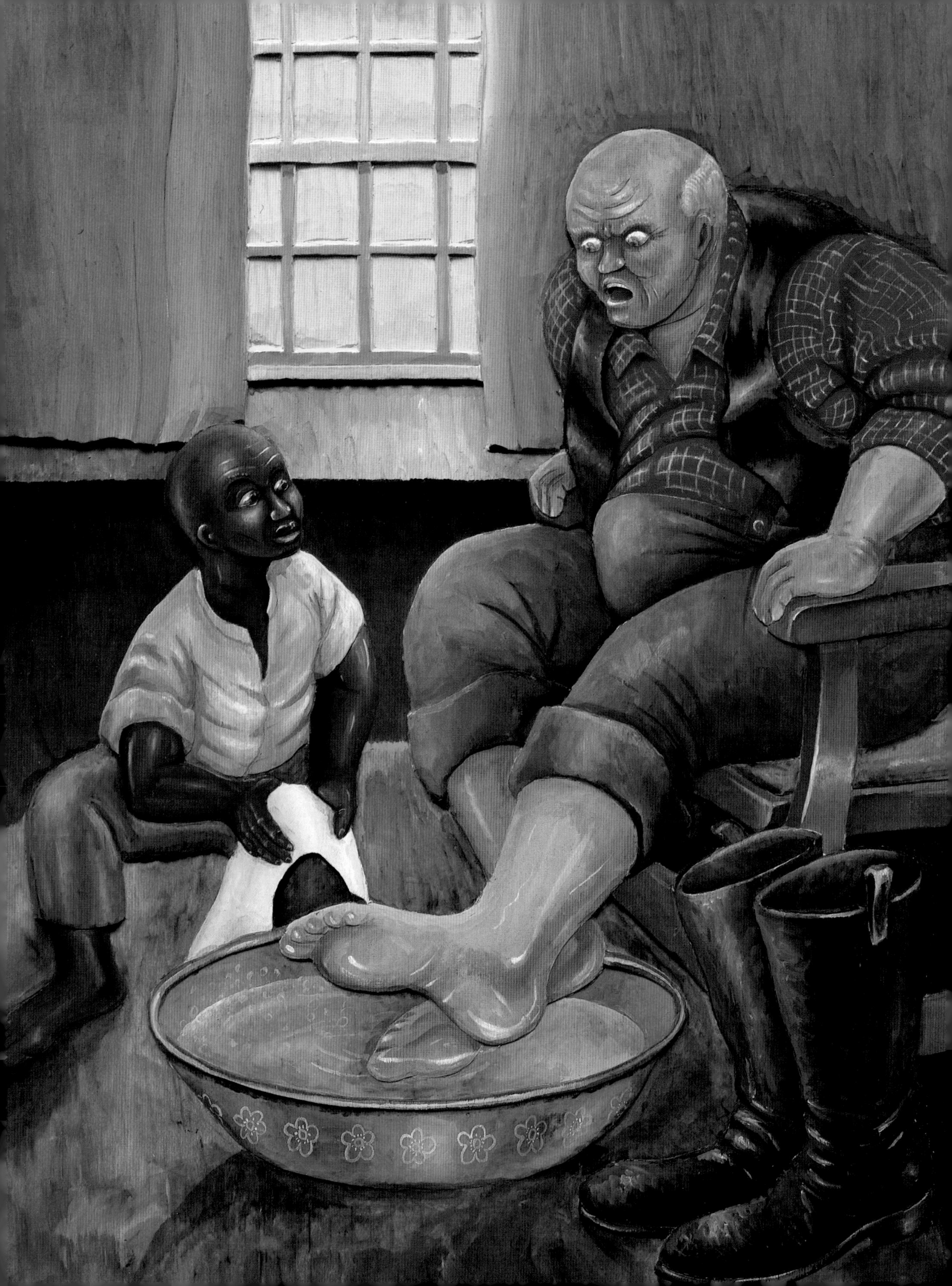

Finally, Hezekiah built up his nerve and said, "Master, you're a betting man. I bet I can tell you the one secret thing that scares you the most. And if I can, will you let me go free?"

"You fool, nothing scares me," Master Thompson said, chuckling. "But I will make a wager with you. If you can tell me anything that scares me, I'll give you a full night's head start. But the next morning, I will come hunting for you with dogs and whips."

Suddenly, Master Thompson thought of all the secrets Hezekiah had already revealed. For a second, the thought sparked a streak of fear in him. But his fear quickly turned to anger, and he lashed out at Hezekiah.

"And I warn you," the master growled, "if you can't tell me of anything that scares me, you'll be Master Wayland's slave after spring auction."

Hezekiah swallowed hard and his small legs trembled. Master Wayland's cruelty was known far and wide. But Hezekiah had vowed to risk his life for freedom, or die trying, and he answered, "Yes, sir, Master Thompson. And you give your word that I get a full night's start?"

"Certainly. You have my word," said the slave master, grinning. You see, Master Thompson believed no one knew his greatest fear. He had never told a living soul.

Then Hezekiah began to describe a summer's eve a long time ago. His voice brought Master Thompson back to a place where he had played as a child and to the day he had found the baby crows.

The sides of Master Thompson's mouth began to twitch involuntarily as he listened and remembered.

Hezekiah kept on, past the end of the crow's tale, for he had learned much as a foot warmer. "On the day you came to see the last bird die, it was gone. You searched for the little bird's dead body, finding not a trace. And that's when you became scared for the first time in your life."

Master Thompson's face drained of color. In surprise and shock, he gasped for air.

Hezekiah's voice grew stronger, "Now, haunting your nights, is the fear that the missing crow will come back to settle the score by clawing out your eyes."

Master Thompson threw up his hands and covered his face. He let out a bloodcurdling howl that could be heard all the way to the edge of his plantation.

And Hezekiah slipped away, knowing he had won the bet.

That very evening, the crow accompanied Hezekiah on the path to freedom, whispering of what Hezekiah would see and do in the free man's land. But late in the night, when the moon shimmered bright on the wet dew, the crow bid Hezekiah farewell, swooping away silently.

Before retiring to bed, Master Thompson's spirits revived and he bragged to his men, "We're going to hunt a slave in a few hours, but first let me take a little nap. That foolish slave thinks I'm going to let him be. Ha! He'll be swinging from a tree before morning."

Later that night, Master Thompson awoke from a nightmare to hear a strange screeching sound filling his bedroom. His feet were cold and trembling without his foot warmer. His heart pounded as his eyes adjusted to the shadows in his moonlit room and his body froze at the sight in the window. Perched on the ledge was a crow, clawing the windowsill, his blackness spilling into the room.

Master Thompson was paralyzed with fear. And, legend has it, he remained ranting and raving in that room until he died.

Even now, on nights when bitter-cold winds rustle through the trees surrounding the old, dilapidated plantation house, some say you can still hear the piercing screams of Master Thompson and see the ghostly silhouette of a crow perched on the windowsill—ensuring that Master Thompson's ghost will never rise to pursue Hezekiah and his descendants.